VS. DRAGON

By Chris Barton
Art by Shanda McCloskey

Little, Brown and Company
New York   Boston

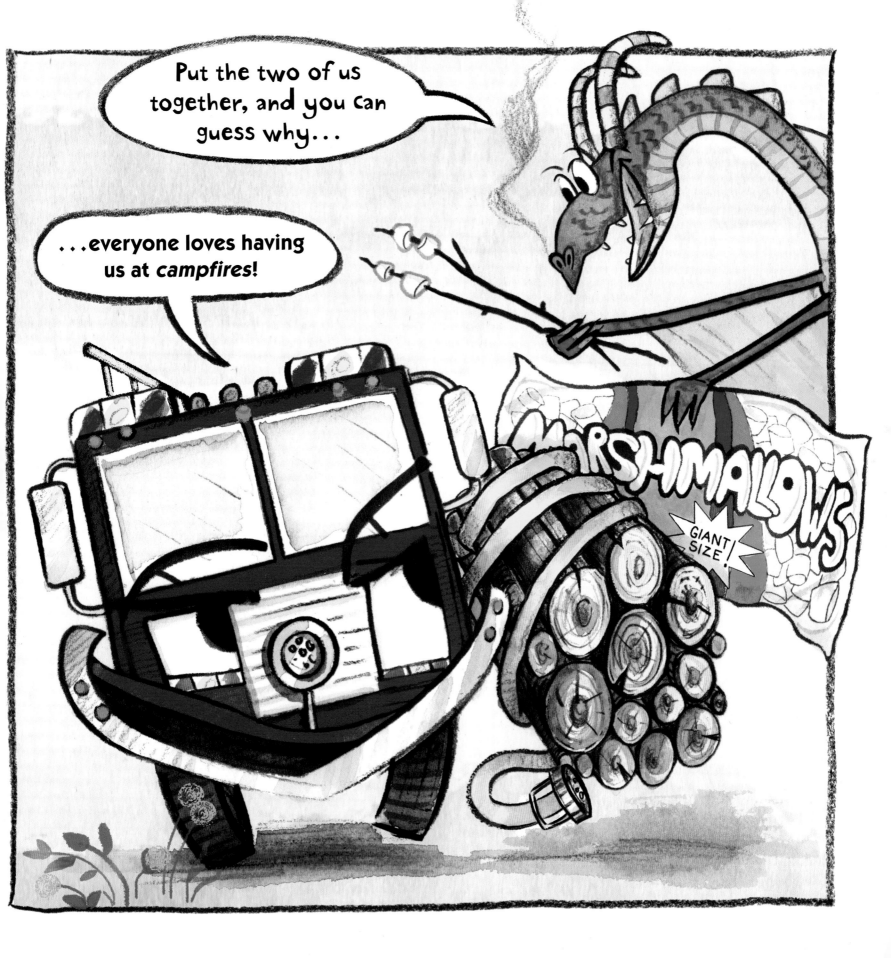

Then...under the midnight moon...a fearsome forest creature appeared!

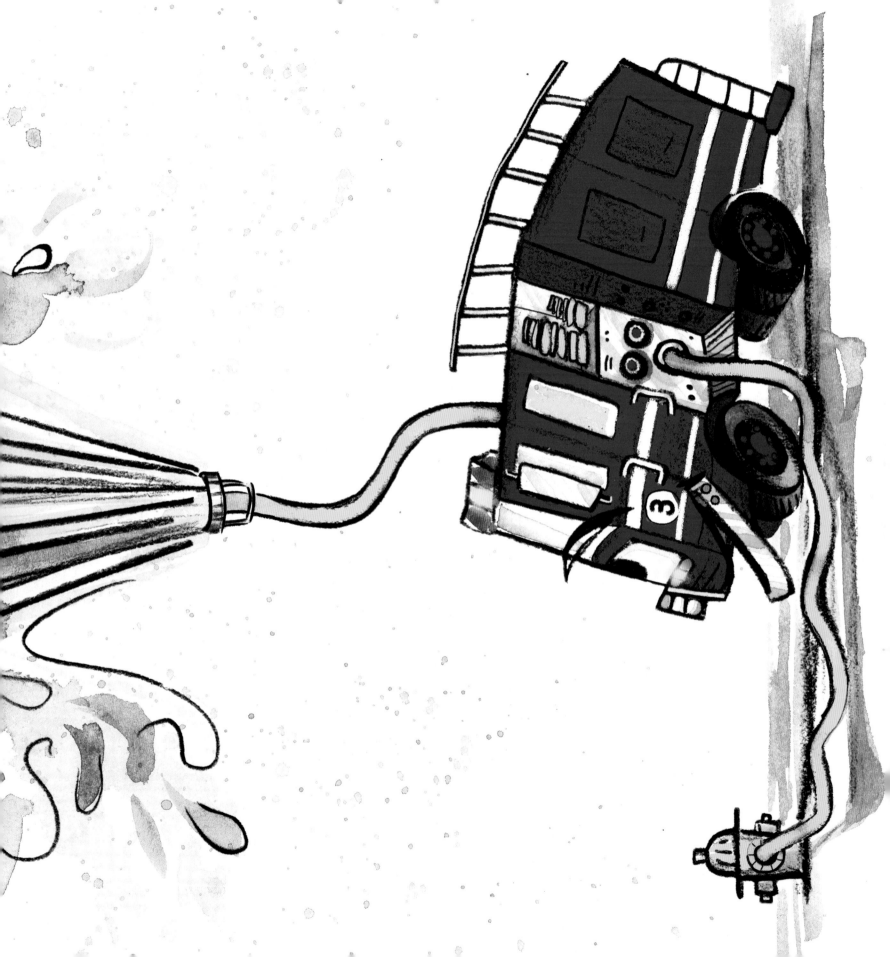

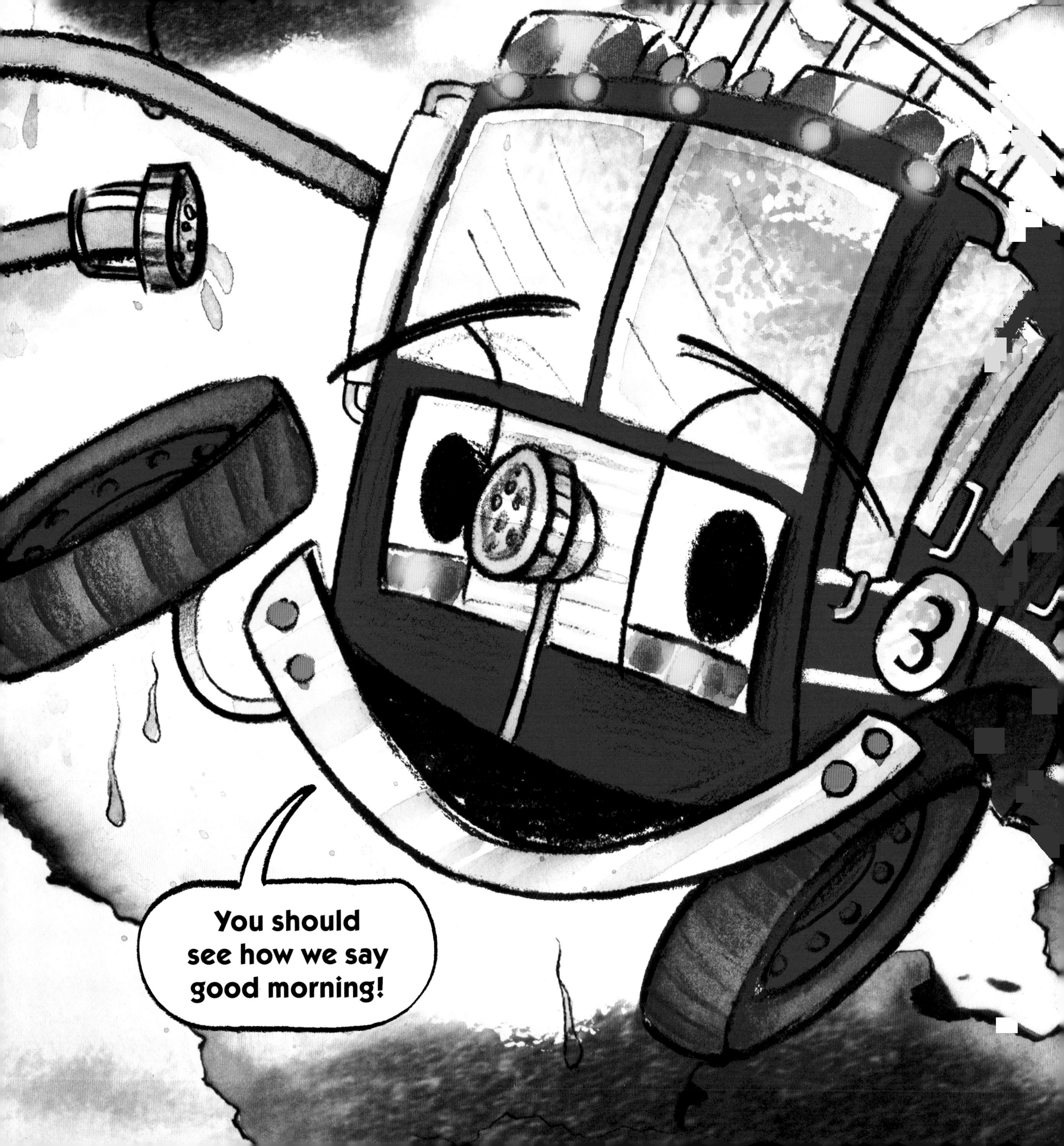
You should see how we say good morning!

For Cynthia Leitich Smith, and all the things
she's really, really, really good at
—CB

For my kids (Harvey Jane and Beni), who also have a
plethora of interesting talents
—SM